WHALE IN THE SKY

WHALE IN THE SKY

by Anne Siberell

A UNICORN BOOK   E. P. DUTTON   NEW YORK

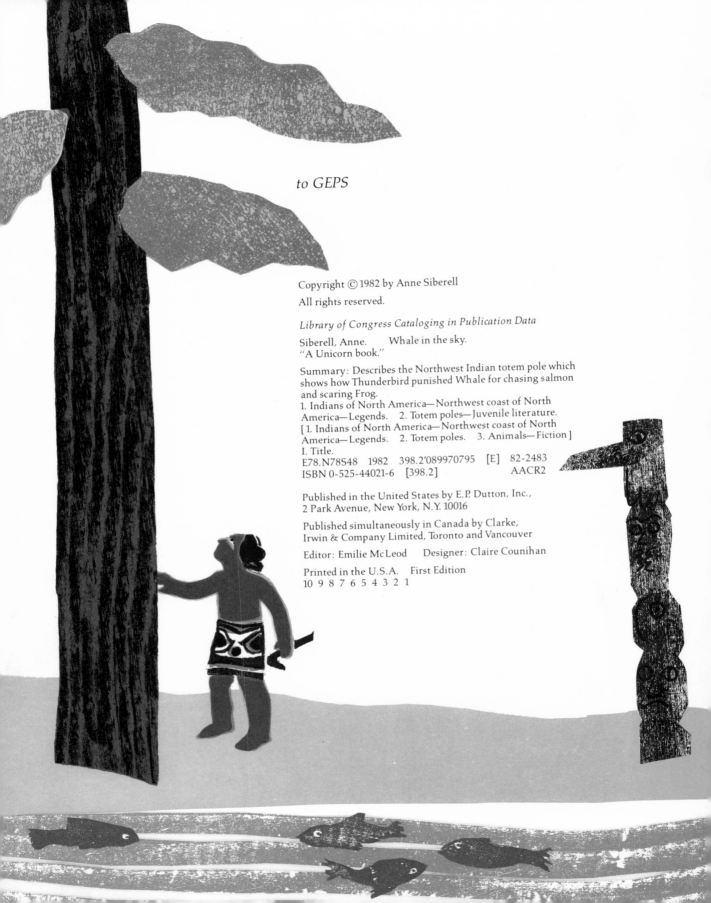

to GEPS

Library of Congress Cataloging in Publication Data

Siberell, Anne.   Whale in the sky.
"A Unicorn book."

Summary: Describes the Northwest Indian totem pole which
shows how Thunderbird punished Whale for chasing salmon
and scaring Frog.
1. Indians of North America—Northwest coast of North
America—Legends.   2. Totem poles—Juvenile literature.
[1. Indians of North America—Northwest coast of North
America—Legends.   2. Totem poles.   3. Animals—Fiction]
I. Title.
E78.N78S48   1982   398.2'089970795   [E]   82-2483
ISBN 0-525-44021-6   [398.2]   AACR2

Published in the United States by E.P. Dutton, Inc.,
2 Park Avenue, New York, N.Y. 10016

Published simultaneously in Canada by Clarke,
Irwin & Company Limited, Toronto and Vancouver

Editor: Emilie McLeod   Designer: Claire Counihan

Printed in the U.S.A.   First Edition
10 9 8 7 6 5 4 3 2 1

Long ago, the rivers and sea were filled with fish, and tall trees crowded the mountainsides. There was no written language among the Indian tribes of the Northwest, and storytellers passed history and legends from one generation to the next. Sometimes a chief would hire an artist to carve a story in pictures on the trunk of a giant tree. *Whale in the Sky* is such a tale.

The carved tree, called a totem pole, identified the chief and his family, his clan and tribe.

In a time long ago, Thunderbird watched over
the sea and land and all its creatures.

One day he saw Whale, small on the horizon
of the sea. He did not see Frog, small on the
bank of the river.

Frog trembled because Whale was growing larger.
The salmon swam faster and faster as Whale chased
them through the sea and into the river.

Whale chased the salmon up the river,
and Frog was afraid.

He called to Raven.

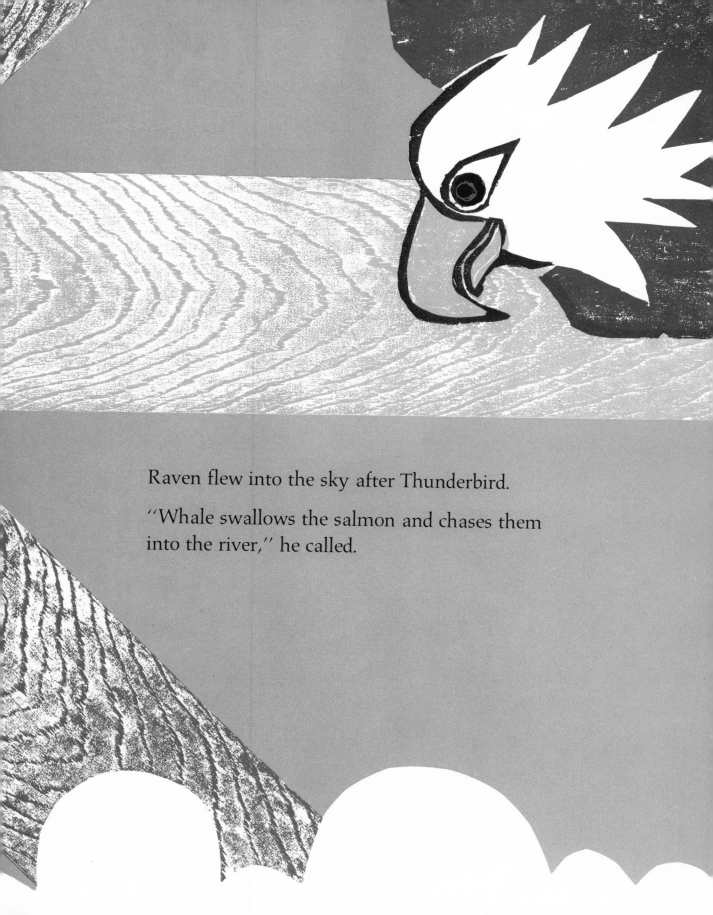

Raven flew into the sky after Thunderbird.

"Whale swallows the salmon and chases them into the river," he called.

Thunderbird stretched his great wings wide
and flew like the wind.

He saw Whale in the river.

He grabbed Whale in his terrible talons and flew
high into the sky. Whale struggled and screamed.

Thunderbird flew higher and higher. Then he
dropped Whale on the highest mountain.

Frog was safe. He thanked his friend Raven.
Now there were salmon for the people
who lived beside the river.

Whale gasped and shivered on the mountain.
He promised to stay out of the river
if he could return to the sea.

Thunderbird clapped his great wings, and
Whale slid down the mountain, back to the sea.

The chief of the people told this tale
to the carver. The carver made the story
into a totem pole.

Thunderbird holds Whale, while Raven
watches over Salmon and Frog.

THE CARVER'S TOOLS

Adzes of jadeite, a hard stone, with wood handles

Wedges   Mallet-like *hammers* of wood   *Chisels* of stone or bone

Rough, dried *sharkskin* for smoothing   *Glue* from boiled halibut fins

Modern totem poles are carved with steel-bladed knives.

COLORS

Black and *gray* were made from charcoal, manganese or graphite, mixed with fish oil, animal oil or chewed salmon eggs.

Brown, from bear dung or chewed cedar bark with oils

Green, copper scraped from rocks and soaked in urine

Yellow, from decayed moss and fungus with oils

Red, from berries and animal blood, mixed with oils

Purple, from berries

Brushes were made from strands of cedar bark or animal fur.

The colors were mixed in stone dishes.

White, from crushed clamshells